AF373591

THE LAST CHORD™ SERIES

Story № 1 : At the edge of the Universe

CONTENTS

DREAM

Tapping his toes with excitement on every step, he was on the way to Qono, his organizer. He finally had the Dream. Not that he did not sleep before, but dreams always avoided Merva. So the significance of the Dream he had could not be overlooked. He needed to be sure. He needed Qono.

Merva was born into a world without animals. He never heard sounds you and I are so used to, my dear reader. He was tall, very tall, among his people. Not like the Tallest One, but quite close. He knew from birth he is destined for something great, at the least to become a protagonist of the story you are reading now. Don't worry, this is not about you though, not even about Merva, as I am sure he will find out soon enough by himself.

Qono was an old and wise organiser. Being one of the Short ones, Qono managed to rise to the top of hierarchy through enormous amounts of determination and by constantly using (and withholding) his wisdom at exactly the right moments. When their world was accepted as a Note of Notes into the harmony of the Last Chord, beings far older than the Tallest One were constantly walking their streets. It is true, height did not matter to them since their patterns grew under completely different circumstances. Seeing that the others started to walk their streets, even though the Tall ones did not really pay attention to them, Tallest One wanted to immediately send a message to the Last Chord requesting dissolution of relations. Qono, to his own amazement, managed to convince the Tallest One not to do so.

The amazement was not unfounded. None of the organisers could EVER convince the Tallest One on any issue. While it could be argued that the Tallest One voiced his dismay as a rouse with his real intent being the test of organisers in the Deep Borrow, such behaviour is unusual, even for the Tallest One. Thus, everyone believed that it was actually Qono who influenced the flow of decisions. And so, Qono finally received respect that, in his view, matched the entirety of his wisdom.

It was the same wisdom that allowed Qono to become the organiser of choice for every young-ling with any height potential. You see, my dear reader, the ground of their world (especially where their cities were created) significantly impeded neural activity. It was said that falling asleep on the ground equalled complete lobotomy. So, obviously the society was heightist. The tallest ruled. The tallest had all the advantages and could make all the decisions.

So, by slowly becoming an organiser of value, the position fed its own importance and someone like Merva was sure to find his way to Qono, empowering Qono even more. As usual, Qono was quietly hanging on the old broken vine of street-lights outside of his dwelling on the edge of the city, the dwelling he refused to leave. At this height he could finally think, even though hanging upside down from a wobbly vine was not a reassuring position. No worry, Qono's position in the Deep Borrow was very much assured. So he relaxed, as much as the hanging allowed him, and contemplated his plans. While having "ear to the ground" hearing and being able to recognise Merva's toe taps from very far away, Qono did not move a muscle, even when Merva was standing right next to him, Merva's head in line with Qono. Merva, being excited and trying to hide his nervousness, spoke:

- I know you can hear me, Qono! Why do
you pretend as if I am not here?

Merva's and Qono's interactions throughout
Merva's life were not entirely pleasant. Qono used to
do the same mental tricks, and you can imagine, my
dear reader, that after a long life of Tall young-ling,
no matter how many tricks you perform, they all
become old. So Merva knew what was to follow and,
with impatience, tapped his toes as Qono continued
his charade:

- Who said I am pretending? You, my
friend, are not really here. Your feet are
all the way down there, on the ground.
Your head is next to me. But you – the
real you – are so far away, you yourself
cannot even imagine.

- Enough with your wit! Do you really
want me to go to another organiser? I
am sure any of them would love to be my
guide!

- I am only here because you came here.
If you wish to go to someone else, I will
not be here once you do.

- Okay, okay! Calm down, Qono. Sheesh!

Merva gathered his breath, which (given his height) took some time, and continued:

- I had a Dream, Qono. I finally had a Dream! I need your help to see if this is my Greatness or if it is me becoming ordinary like everyone else.

- Oh, a Dream? How do you know? What was it about?

- Come on, Qono! Do you not know the rules? I am not supposed to share my Dream with anyone! Otherwise my decisions will not be my own any more!

- Well, if you do not want to share your Dream with me, what do you want me to do then?

Qono turned toward Merva. His eyes peered deep into Merva's eyes. He almost managed to see the constellations of the Last Chord dimly reflecting on the surface of huge middle eye of Merva. Merva was not blinking. His eyes were open to the Great High and he seemed ready to accept his destiny. He lifted his foot and pressed it against the wall of Qono's dwelling. The vine broke on the far end and snapped down, smashing Qono against the wall. Qono jumped down and stared up, with anger. Merva immediately reacted:

- I am sorry, Qono. I did not mean to ruin your height exercises. But I really need to know how to find out whether it is Greatness or whether I am becoming like everyone else!

- Well, that is so obvious, is it not?

Deep within, Qono was really enjoying this moment. He continued:

- Do I really have to spell it out for you? Do you think you are destined for any kind of Greatness if you cannot even see this? I am going to ask you. What do you need to do in order to find out whether it is a REGULAR DREAM?

Qono jumped up, holding onto the vine, climbing toward the roof of his dwelling. He was not even going to wait for Merva's reply down there. He puffed as climbing took allot out of Short ones.

Merva looked up, thinking for a moment and smashed his head against the wall of Qono's dwelling, exclaiming:

> - Oh! How could I not see this! You are right, Qono! You are so right!

- I clearly am, though you are trying to destroy my dwelling again! Is that the thanks I get for my help? Never mind... So what do you need to do in order to know?

Merva, impatiently waited until Qono finished, and said:

> - Go to sleep again! Once I sleep some more, if I do not dream, then the Dream is one of a kind and so am I. If, however I have another dream as soon as I sleep, I am just diminishing and becoming like everyone else.

- Good! Now go, leave me in peace!

Qono concentrated all of his attention to reattaching the vine to the far end of the roof. Merva was already running away, shouting in the darkness:

- Thanks, Qono! Thank you so much! I will let you know what I find out!

Qono, puffing with exertion, mumbled to himself:

- You should. Don't bother me with useless issues though. Next time, come with something concrete and important.

But Merva surely did not hear that. He would not hear it even if he was still standing next to Qono, just as he did in the beginning of the conversation. He has decided. And he was rushing toward the execution.

INVESTIGATION

Merva now needed to find a place to sleep. Tall ones had problems sleeping as part of normal cycle. There was no sun that made the time visibly pass on their world by differentiating Day and Night like Sol on Earth. So sleeping was not a part of daily cycles. Sleeping was induced by chants or certain thoughts. And for Tall ones it required staying completely still and locking all their knee joints. Because they could not lay their head on the ground or anything else built of the same material that penetrated their entire world.

Tall ones slept by strengthening their legs and locking their three knee joints, spreading their three feet around to make up a pyramid. Then they would either chant or look up to the stars in the sky, trying to figure out the orientation and motion path of their world as it hurled itself through the Universe. Either way they would eventually sleep. But for Merva, full of excitement, sleep was not easy to achieve. His thoughts would constantly interrupt his chants and would definitely not allow him to concentrate on any of the stars in the sky above. Not even the most distant ones – and those were usually easy, as all Merva would have to do is squint. You see, my dear reader, inhabitants of that world had eyes that were maid to explore the heavens. We, on Earth, use lenses and radio circuits to explore the Universe, because with our naked eyes we can only see so far. Tall ones (and even Short ones for that matter) never required such things. Almost like us, they could focus their eyes very precisely on any distance away from them. Unlike us, they could also tighten their field of vision, significantly enlarging anything they are looking at. Imagine standing on your balcony, looking at the moon with the naked eye and being able to differentiate between two particles of moon dust on the surface there. This sort of skill was quite ordinary among the Short ones. Tall ones were even better since they had more eyes and their eyes were much larger. But I digress. Merva needed to concentrate in order to squint and he could not muster the mental power while trying not to forget a single tiniest detail of his Dream. He could postpone the entire investigation and let sleep come when it comes, but he has learned one trait from Qono – persistence.

So Merva, not willing to give up, was moving from one spot to another in their city, locking his knees and trying to sleep again and again with no avail. Sleep eluded him. And, by the rules of the Tallest Ones set throughout the ages, he was not permitted to even think about his first ever Dream before finding out whether he was destined for Greatness or just becoming like all the other Tall ones. Because, while his memory was only growing at the time, there was no assurance that he will still remember the Dream fully by the time he finds out his destiny and is able to think about his Dream.

Qono, meanwhile, was already on his way to Deep Borrow as it was time to consolidate his influence. He already knew the answer to Merva's search, and, by sending Merva out to sleep – knowing full well Merva would not be able to do so – Qono bought himself enough time to place all of the pawns in the right places. His ambition would finally pay off.

It was quite uneasy, though quite usual, for the Short ones to attempt to run. Their feet were the same size as the Tall ones, but their legs were much shorter and one (or in some cases even two!) of them missed a knee joint. They did not cry, though. The hardships of survival under the darkness of the sky coupled with problems of their physical build, made them perfect organisers. They would always know where to build and where to destroy. Where to save and where to abandon. Where to use and where to disregard. And they would know stars.

Their knowledge of stars was born through the ages of their world. Being short, they longed for the heavens so much, they studied it most of all. They took study of the heavens far beyond the level of best cosmologists of Earth. They were almost ready to figure out the reality of the entire universe when the subject got forbidden by the Tallest One. It is through their study the world got discovered and then accepted into the Last Chord. Qono proudly felt the acceptance, even though being the prize for many Short ones, was his own doing, his alone. And now he was finally going to attempt the unthinkable. His pattern allowed him to concentrate on his goals the same way Merva would concentrate on a star in the heavens. Nothing else mattered as long as the goal was achieved in the end. Short ones took the basic determination interwoven into Tall ones' patterns and polished it to perfection. But I guess that is the law throughout the Universe – the harder our life is the more we work to improve it. Qono's mind right now was concentrating on one thing – the entry into the hall of Deep Borrow. He reached the centre of the city and started his walk around the huge tall spire, regulating his breathing repeatability to the nanosecond and searching for most comfortable vine of lights.

He also had to look up as he walked since there was no star to their world and Tall ones did not produce shadows. If a Tall one would step on him by mistake, it would break his concentration and he would have to start all over again. The ritual had to be completed once in its entirety, otherwise Qono would not be able to reach the hall. He finally found the suitable vine and started climbing. Keeping his knee-less leg away to the side, he was holding on to the vine and rhythmically moving his two other legs, in line with his steady breathing. The climb was very long. His entire existence he was waiting for this moment so he was absolutely determined not to ruin it by haste. Steady pace, steady breathing, steady mind. Concentrate. Don't look up. Don't look down. Don't look to the sides. Look at your feet, make sure the step is steady and the grip is there. Do not think of anything else. Step. Step. Ste...

Merva finally found a place where he was able to look up and see no stars. He squinted so much it hurt, and still there was nothing. Sleep was coming. Merva felt his concentration drifted away, slowly.

He... will... sleep... at last...

Strange object shimmered into existence relatively nearby, glancing by his field of vision and then overtaking it, seemingly appearing out of nowhere. The object was large and had so much detail to it that Merva almost lost consciousness. Merva shook off sleepy thoughts and widened his eyes. The object was definitely closing in. Others used such objects for travel and Merva could not widen his eyes fast enough to see the relative motion of things and to realise what was going to happen.

Qono felt a tremor in the vine as the tension suddenly released. He grabbed the vine harder and pulled more, but to no avail. He was falling. His gaze shifted upwards when he saw a huge vessel (probably full of the others) gliding by slowly and scraping away the hall of Deep Borrow, missing the Tallest One by mere foot. Tallest One was sleeping and obviously did not realise what was going on. At this time, only three Short ones were climbing the Deep Borrow and they were falling as well. Qono could probably recognise them if he wanted to but he was just so happy they were falling down too that the thought did not even enter his mind. There was only one thing that would make this situation happier for Qono – if at the moment of impact Gumta was in the hall on top. Qono stored this investigation for later. Right now his intent was to find at least one vine that is still attached to the hall up above.

As most of the Tall ones in the city were asleep, blindly gazing at the heavens, none of them got disturbed by the arrival of the object. Merva accurately left his spot and started running towards the Deep Borrow. He was already able to see that mostly things were fine and no one got really hurt, but Merva had abundance of curiosity in him and thus continued running. The object was floating away, apparently grabbed by the world's distortion of space-time and entering orbit while tumbling around.

Running by the Deep Borrow, Merva noticed Qono, above his head.

> - Are you okay, Qono? Do you need any help?

- Why do you care so much? Don't you need to continue following that thing?

Qono moved his eyes pointing toward the object. He really needed Merva to be busy right now and could not let events unfolding interfere with his plans. But Merva was just standing there. Qono had to be careful:

- Look, Merva. You need to concentrate on your investigation and I need to concentrate on mine. This is the way things work on our world. You know this as well as me, so do not worry about this old Short one, I will be fine. Do what you need to do. What you are driven to do.

> – Okay, Qono! But afterwards I am going to pass by and still see if you need any help, deal?

– Deal, deal! Now go!

Merva turned around and continued running away after the object as it was closing with the horizon. Merva liked running. After watching the stars it was his second favourite thing to do. If not for his destiny, whichever it might be, Merva would just keep running around the world, looking upwards into the heavens. He would not stumble, he could not. He has three legs, like all the rest, only they treated their steps as unsteady. The only one who was completely sure in his steps was the Tallest One. That is why Merva thought he is destined for Greatness when the time comes. So Merva continued running after the object.

Qono, after managing to find a vine that was still attached, started climbing again. The Deep Borrow thinned up allot toward the top, and the hall was so tiny that someone like Qono needed to put all his feet together and his toes would still hang out over the edge. But such were the rules. You could only discuss things with the Tallest One when you are at the hall of Deep Borrow. Otherwise he would not consider your input and would not consider you as well for that matter. So while only one can be up there, the rest would have to hang on the vines and wait their turn. And Tallest One had to be fair so every Short one climbing the vines would have to be heard. If you are released you have to step down.

But now Tallest One was sleeping and the only fight around Deep Borrow was for the place of being the first to talk to when Tallest One wakes up. And at the moment the hall was swiped off by the passing object, so Qono needed to hurry. Qono, to his own surprise, managed to catch and steady his breath. He recovered quite quickly (obviously training at home helped here allot) and continued the climb. He could hear the steps on the other side of the Deep Borrow. They were a bit below. So Qono picked up the tempo. He chanted to himself and concentrated. Step by step. Up and up. Step by step. Up and up. Step by step. Up and up... Qono finally reached the top of the Deep Borrow and climbed over the edge to stand there. But since the object just swiped the top off the Deep Borrow the hall was now wider, and, to Qono's dismay, there was a hand grabbing the edge on the other side. The other Short one climbed up. It was Gumta!

Come to think of it, Qono was well prepared for it to be Gumta and was not at the least surprised. Qono was very strategic in dispensing his wisdom around, while Gumta seemed to have no strategy behind his actions at all. He was just lucky. He obviously was smart enough to agree at the end of his speech with whatever Tallest One decides, and even, at times, predict Tallest One's decision and making him think he was led to it by Gumta. What a vile pretender! So if destruction and rearrangement of Deep Borrow hall was not enough, it would have obviously be Gumta to try and take advantage of the situation.

Qono could not imagine Gumta's decisions from any other point of view. Patterns of organisers were too one-dimensional to be able to imagine someone else's point of view. That is why Tallest Ones always chose an organiser to be an advisor to their rule. Tallest Ones had a destiny of making important decisions while Short ones were left to deal with the consequences of those. The Deep Borrow hall was instituted long before Qono's and Gumta's time.

It was an attempt to overthrow societal order led by a friendship developed between a Tall one and a Short one that prompted Tallest Ones to create the single Deep Borrow. On one hand it gave a minimal opportunity to the Short ones to be heard (as if the Tallest One would ever really listen) and on the other end honed the Short ones' struggle to the direction of servitude and inner squabbles rather than making them think for themselves and form any kind of political movement.

My dear reader, do not for a moment think that servitude of the organisers on that world meant anything similar to the servitude on Earth. Short ones were by no means oppressed. Tall ones (and Short ones) did not need or want anything that related to physical survival. Their patterns continued without end unless they by themselves decided to disappear. The only currency on their world was need to exist. If Short one or Tall one had lost their need to exist they would seize to be. So, from completely sociological perspective, if Short ones created their own political movement and at some point decided not to serve as organisers any more at least some of them would end up loosing their meaning and thus their will to exist.

As carriers of wisdom on their world, no single Short one would ever listen to another Short one. As for listening to the Tall one – forget it. Because of this, for Short ones who lost their will to exist, there would be no help. They would immediately disappear and turn into pure energy. Short ones blessed the first Shortest One for discovering that Tall ones actually existed. Before that discovery, it was thought that the feet moving on the ground were from one single celestial creature that very long time ago swallowed their world and now moved it inside its stomach with these "feet".

Managing the Tall ones' desire to exist was even more difficult. They could see the universe around their world and could peer into the vastness of space-time unaffected by the clouds of dust below their knees. As such, very early on, they learned of their own insignificance compared to the Universe, which brought them into the state of deep and perpetual depression. That depression could not be cured unless they found the meaning to their existence. But they could not build or create because of their height. So physical world below was far beyond reach, way too far, especially for the Tallest Ones. But this story is not about the past. It is about the future of our heroes and their real purpose in the Universe.

If you wish to know more about the history of their world I would invite you, my dear reader, to visit the lost planes on the other side of their planet. There, between the halls of the past, you would for sure find records of previous events. Here, however, all you need to take from our little excursion into history is that their race (and they are of the same race, mind you) created very precarious cultural symbiosis. Any break of that symbiosis would end the existence of their society in whole and of each and every one of them separately.

So by all means, when Humanity acquires its deep-space legs and the world of our heroes is found, I invite you, my dear reader, to be the first to journey to the lost planes of history and uncover all the hidden subjects and all the realities of Tall vs Short existence. For now, though, you would simply have to take my word for it – even if my understanding of their social dynamic is entirely wrong.

THE DUEL

This was unheard of. When Tallest One wakes up from his sleep, he would have to decide who to listen to first. Both Qono and Gumta were highly admired by the Tallest One and he would never be able to decide which one of them to listen to first. Prior to the incident the Tallest One had only one organiser at any point in time. The others would wait and the queue was naturally controlled by the order of their arrival to the top. This incident, however stirred the order of things, apparently in the wrong direction. Now, both Qono and Gumta stood on top of the Deep Borrow in the middle of the new hall. They had to quickly decide what to do or their world would plunge into catastrophe. For a very long time no Short one interacted with another unless it was through their influence of a common Tall one. But even that was done in a serial manner, not in parallel.

It was only obvious that neither Qono nor Gumta was about to let go of their place at the hall. If both of them did, they could, together, chamfer the edges of the hall so there was only one standing place and restore the order of things for the common good. But the patterns of Short ones were, as you understand by now, incredibly selfish. So working together was out of the question. They stared at each other, motionless and stunned, the way a deer would peer into the lights of approaching car. While their wisdoms were raging inside them, they missed a crucial point of the situation – Unba, the Tallest One, woke up. Blinking periodically with one of his many eyes, Unba stared at the hall of Deep Borrow in total silence. Through his entire long life after his Dream there was always a Short one that would start talking to him even before he would open his eyes. He never had to choose a topic of conversation. But now, waking up to total silence, Unba started to feel uneasy. He decided to wait and see what will happen at the hall of Deep Borrow before opening his mouth.

While this whole situation might look comical to you, my dear reader, if it were to continue for very much longer, the echelon of power on their world would crumble and disappear. To their luck, however, an interruption showed up on the horizon. Merva was running back, arriving from the opposite end of their planet. He had completed the chase and saw what happened with the object that so irreversibly changed the balance of power on their world.

Merva, used to constant rumble of Unba's voice at the Deep Borrow, was quite surprised to witness the situation developing at the hall. Usually, if Qono was the one on top, Merva would have to wait until Unba released Qono. Now, however, especially with his Dream on the line, Merva spoke first:

- Unba, Qono ! Listen to what I have found! I saw the others! So many of them! I have never seen this kind of activity before!

Gumta immediately saw a way to move forward and snatch Merva at the same time, but before he could open his mouth, Qono asked:

- It was a ship, wasn't it? Did the others land at the planes of history? How many of them?

- They did not! They ignored our world completely. You are right, Qono, it was a ship. But it was empty. That is why it was tumbling around and that is why it has scraped off the hall of Deep Borrow here.

Merva caught his breath and continued, while Unba, Qono and Gumta listened intently:

- They did not land on our world. Another ship appeared nearby, many of them left that ship, moving through space in their strange outer shells. They got into the second ship and took it away. They all left!

Gumta finally did bud in, trying to hijack the attention of Unba:

- Excellent news! Thanks, Merva! I have always supported Unba's decision to stop interacting with the others. They bring only trouble and disarray with them! I, for once, am very happy they left. Do you agree, Unba?

- I do, Gumta! Such disregard for our sovereignty has to be acted on! I am going to send a message to the Last Chord now. The others need to leave our world and never come back! We have nothing for them here, it has been well established, so there is no need for them to be here.

Gumta grinned at Qono, who spoke quite rapidly:

- Unba, why did the ship appear here? If we are of no use to the others, why send a ship? I, for once, would like to know why. I completely understand that it is not in the best interest of the Tallest One to explore and enquire because you do have a world to run, Unba. But, perhaps you could send someone on your behalf. Do you think Gumta is up to the task? He is the most eager to serve among all of the Short ones.

Gumta's mouth closed into a tight little dot of anger. I assume you are familiar with the current theories of black holes, my dear reader. Because the amount of pressure at the edge of Gumta's mouth was very close to the forces that create black holes throughout the cosmos. But at the back of his mind, Gumta was still. He knew his strategy would eventually work out. So he stayed quiet. Unba, however spoke, raising his voice in anger and astonishment:

> - No, Qono! For the millionth time NO! Our place is on our world. We will do no such thing!

Gumta's expression changed into a tiny portrait of bliss. He was finally winning, after such a long annoyance with Qono's interruptions of his plans. "At last, Unba will be able to choose the Shortest One" – he thought to himself. Merva, however, spoke suddenly:

> - Unba! Qono! Gumta! Are you not listening to me? The others left their other ship next to our world! It is quite larger than the one that scraped the hall of Deep Borrow! And, as far as I can figure out, it is in our path!!! If we do not do something, we will smash straight into it and there will be no world for you to run, Unba! If you wish to stay here and send messages to the Last Chord feel free to do so! I am going to the planes of history to see if I can do something!

Merva, angrily looking at Qono with all of his eyes, asked:

- Are you with me, Qono? Or do you want to stay here and debate some more?

Qono had to consider everything. If Merva was right – and we all know that Tall ones are not very trustworthy with their astronomical orientation – the world was in danger. A ship of the others bigger than the last one? That would definitely be a cataclysm. If, however the ship does not destroy the world, Qono would be ridiculed by Unba, and Gumta will surely spread the news to the rest of the Tall ones. Qono might be even forbidden to ever climb the Deep Borrow again! He had to decide one way or the other and take the consequences when they come. Qono shook the deeper thoughts off and said, energetically:

- I am with you, Merva. But you better be right! How long do we have?

- Not long, I suggest you jump on me as I am much faster runner than you are, my friend!

Qono gave a hard stare to Unba and jumped off the

Deep Borrow as Merva closed his eyes. Landing on Merva's eyelid, Qono slid down to one of his many dimples and grabbed Merva's short fur with both of his hands. Merva took off with haste. The planes of history were on the other side of the world and getting there was not easy. Merva already fell almost twice when following the ship. He, however, developed a running style on the way back to the Deep Borrow that seemed to work on their world. He was taking long jumps from one leg to another, and by the time he returned to his first leg he would cover about twenty of his lengths. That new style of locomotion even made wind run through his fur. He discovered he liked the feeling. But now he did not have the time to enjoy it. He had to concentrate and not fall down. Counting in his mind "one, two, three, one, two, three, one, two, three" Merva ran in complete silence.

Qono was holding on tight and his head, unlike Merva's, was full with thoughts. What would they find in the planes of history? He only took a journey there once in search of the origins of the Shortest one, back when he was trying to get to the vines of Deep Borrow for the first time. What will they do when they reach the planes? What can they do against such forces in the Universe?

Meanwhile, back at the hall of Deep Borrow, Unba was making his governing decisions:

- Gumta, listen carefully!

- Yes, Unba?

- Tell all of your Tall ones – I know you organise many of them – to grab the ground with their feet as hard as possible and not to let go under ANY circumstances! Brace, brace for impact! I am doing the same! Go!

Gumta, happy for the outcome with regards to Qono, jumped down, almost recklessly, catching the vine of lights and sliding all the way to the ground. He was the only Short one with three knee joints in tact, so he could run. And run he did. Going from dwelling to dwelling, through the entire city, passing Unba's orders to every Tall one under his wing. If the world does not survive, at least what remains will have his power base and his power base only. All the rest be damned.

Unba, in the meanwhile, concentrated very hard on the Last Chord. If it was his role to communicate with the others, he would leave them such a message, that the entire Universe will shatter in its wake. Tall ones could affect space-time at the point of their concentration. And Unba, being the Tallest One, could do so very far away. Bending to his will, droplets of black and red liquid appeared over the floor at the lobby of the main building for Lost Chord committee. When they finally fell down and splashed a message it read (and I translate it vaguely) "LEAVE US THE ... ALONE, YOU BASTARDS!" - you can replace the three dots with the ugliest and most vile swear word you know and even that would not come close to the actual untranslatable meaning. The message would stay there past the end of the Universe and, with Tallest One's space-time bending abilities, perhaps it is there even now. I would not know, since the Last Chord would only form in the very far future...

THE PLANES OF HISTORY

It is quite important to note that, while tumbling through space in rather random manner, the motion of the world on which our heroes reside did have defined rotational axis. One pole of these axis would pass through the Tallest One's lair, while the other would pass somewhere through the lost planes of history. You see, my dear reader, Tall ones were just too tall to safely exist on the equator as centrifugal forces would throw them out to space if they were not extremely careful. So they had to live on the poles. Mind you, the poles were not North and South as the planet did not have any magnetic field left (not that it needed any, tumbling at the edge of the universe).

The precession of the axis of their planet was so erratic that only the Shortest one, the wisest of the organisers, would be able to predict the motion of their world about an hour ahead. However, none knew where the Shortest one disappeared to. He could have lost his reason to exist and vanish or, perhaps, he could have found a suitable dwelling along the equator, where no Tall one would bother him any more. In any case, no matter where the Shortest one is at the moment, it was his idea to start building Borrows. Short ones always wanted to know what is there, up above, beyond the dust blanket of the sky. Thus, he discovered the Tall ones and made contact with the Tallest One, setting up their society and giving reason to exist and prosperity to every Short and Tall one out there. His first Borrow still stood strong in the middle of the lost planes of history, lost between thousands of other Borrows built by his kind. Lost and unmarked like the Shortest one himself.

Tall ones, as I have mentioned before, did not have any knowledge of the Short ones. Their feet were grabbing the ground as hard as they possibly could, under the floating dust that grabbing produced. They were aimlessly walking around the world, high and mighty, looking at the heavens with awe and amazement. While they were able to see very far and concentrate on remote corners of the vast cosmos, their prediction powers and their wisdom were almost non-existent. And, because of inability to predict and realise the physics of their world, some of them would constantly loose their grasp of the ground around equatorial regions and float into space. Once out, they could survive for some time, as they did not really need air, being as tall as they are with their heads reaching the troposphere, which was quite thinned out. But, in the grand dimensions of the space-time itself, this survival was merely a moment and they would eventually seize to exist. That discouraging situation ended when the first of the Tallest Ones met the Shortest one at the top of the first Borrow.

Many Borrows were built by the Short ones since then, and Tall ones finally found out what was going on beneath the dust and in the sky above. They also found out about the physics of their world and learned not to wander to the equatorial regions. They grew in numbers and prospered greatly, but all of a sudden the Shortest one disappeared. His disappearance took entire world by surprise and entire society was stunned. It took a meteor shower to wake everybody up. The Borrows were pounded by the hail of space rocks as their world plunged into the remnants of past destruction. But as their world survived the cataclysm of its' own star system, it ploughed through this one with relative ease. Their tiny world was one tough nugget, after all. By collective decision – the first ever in their history – they decided to move to the other side of the planet and rebuild the city there. Migration was quick and the old city was forgotten and forbidden, given its' eternal name – the planes of history. The planes of history was the Merva's destination right now. Merva and Qono had to get there fast if they were to do anything to save their world from total destruction.

Borrows of the planes of history appeared at the horizon. Qono could now see them clearly, hanging for his dear life between Merva's huge eyes. But the planes, no matter how attractive to Qono, could not grab his attention fast enough to win over the size of massive space rig hanging above their heads, even as Merva was running. The rig was so much bigger than their world! Qono suddenly realised that when the impact occurs, the rig would hardly suffer any damage at all! And the collision seemed inevitable.

Qono juggled some rough assessments in his head and screamed through the roar of the wind that resulted from Merva's running:

- Merva! Do NOT stop! Run to the tallest
of the Borrows! Run up the slope to the
hall on top and jump up as hard as you
can! We should reach that ship before
the impact!

> - Are you out of your mind? I will not be
> able to catch on! My hands are not
> strong enough and my feet will be
> behind me!

Merva almost stopped in shock. He liked his world
and the Tall ones were taught never to let it go. As I
have told you, my dear reader, heir height would
sometimes allow them to float off into space. He had
a very good friend long time ago, Yoha, who,
according to rumours, disappeared into space
precisely because he did not hold on. Jumping up for
the Tall one was unthinkable! And jumping up from
the hall on top of a Borrow? That would be sure
suicide!

Merva did not need to breath in space, he could
deal with lack of atmosphere for a very long time,
but even that time would eventually pass, and,
instead of vanishing into nothing like any other self-

respecting inhabitant of their world at the end of their journey, Merva would float in space for eternity, a lifeless, motionless piece of space-junk. At that point any onlooker would easily mistake Merva for a tiny meteor, not even worth an iota of attention. But Qono continued:

- Listen to me, Merva! Do not worry, my hands are strong enough! I will grab the ship once we jump, but I cannot get there on my own! And we for sure cannot do a single thing if you do not jump! So, jump, jump up!

- Okay, my friend! Get ready!

Merva quickly looked around, spreading his field of vision all the way to find the highest Borrow. He zeroed in on one. Took several leaps and – to the envy of any basketball star on Earth – jumped up. As Merva's feet left the ground, Qono was already taking in as much air as he possibly could. Once they left the atmosphere, Qono relaxed, loosened the grip of his right hand and let go. He floated next to Merva, grabbing Merva with his left hand, making way towards the space rig. There were many places he could catch on. Qono was not afraid. He calmly scanned the irregular surface of the spaceship in front of them until he saw a spot which reminded him of the opening in the ship that others used when first visiting their world. The spot was approaching so he extended his hands out as much as he could and grabbed the handle next to the pressure equalisation chamber.

The handle turned and the chamber opened. The turn, however released the atmosphere trapped inside and Qono's fingers slid off the handle. The situation was far from optimal, obviously, but at least Merva and Qono would still have enough air in them to witness the carnage from orbit.

Qono, holding onto Merva with all his strength, frantically waved his right hand from side to side trying to grab anything as they were skimming past the surface of the giant space rig...